MW00814184

Unspeakable Lies

By

ALICE TRIBUE

Lynette,
Hope you enjoy Unspeakable
Lies! Luca + Everly
forever!
          -xoxo-
          Alice Tribue

Copyright

Photos by Lindee Robinson Photography

Cover Designed by Najla Qamber Designs

Models: Ahmad Kawsan & Natalie Light

Editing by Editing4Indies
https://www.facebook.com/editing4indies
Formatting by CP Smith

Other Titles
by
Alice Tribue

Dedication

For the awesome readers who asked for more Luca and Everly this is for you.

Prologue

"Tyler, do you take Everly to be your lawfully wedded wife, to have and to hold from this day forward, for better or for worse, for richer, for poorer, in sickness and in health, until death do you part?"

"I do," declares Tyler, his deep voice cracking slightly.

My own eyes are now moist with the threat of unshed tears. His beautiful smile shines down on me, making the butterflies in my stomach take flight. I turn my head to the priest as he begins to speak again.

"Everly, do you take Tyler to be your lawfully wedded husband, to have and to hold from this day forward, for better or for worse, for richer, for poorer, in sickness and in health, until death do you part?"

"I do," I agree, joyfully tilting my head up and looking into Tyler's chocolate brown eyes, the tears pooled in them reflecting my own. This is the kind of moment that every girl dreams of, the happily ever after that we read about when we're little.

"You have declared your consent before the Church. May the Lord in his goodness

1

strengthen your consent and fill you both with blessings. What God has joined let no man divide. Do you have the rings?"

Tyler nods, turning around and taking the rings from his best man. As he turns, I take in the sight of him; really look at this man standing before me. I love the way he looks in his black suit and tie. Tyler is slender with lean, well-defined muscles. His light brown hair is short and perfectly groomed for the occasion. Tyler likes to look good; he's always so well put together. He takes pride in his appearance—even in sweats and a t-shirt he looks styled to perfection. He's tall; so tall that he hovers over me. Even in the highest heels I could find, I still have to look up at him. His thin lips and perfectly chiseled nose make him look almost like the typical boy next door.

I focus on Tyler as he shakily picks up my left hand and grins as he slides a platinum diamond band on my finger.

"With this ring, I thee wed," he says softly, so low that no one past the first few rows likely heard him.

I wipe away a stray tear then turn to my maid of honor who hands me his ring and turn back to Tyler. I take his hand in mine repeating the same words he's just spoken.

"With this ring, I thee wed."

"You place these rings upon each other's fingers as a visible sign of your vows this day. And now by the power vested in me by the state of New Jersey, I hereby pronounce you husband and wife. Tyler," the priest calls with a smile on his face, "you may kiss your bride."

His lips crush down hard against mine and my arms wrap around his neck as cheers erupt throughout the church. Two hundred of our closest friends and family attend, but I don't see any of them. I barely register the fact that they're here at all. The only thing I know is that we did it—that, as of this moment, I'm Tyler's wife and he's my husband. Mine. And this is the day I've been waiting for since I met him on campus four years ago.

We slowly break apart, and I swear it feels more like a fantasy than reality. Tyler looks down at me with his perfect smile and whispers, "I love you, Mrs. West."

"I love you, Mr. West." I giggle as he takes my hand to lead me down the rose-covered aisle and out of the church. Life with Tyler hasn't always been perfect, it hasn't always been easy, but my life is so much better with him in it. I've never doubted his love—not once. He's steady, grounded, and focused; that's what I love about him and Tyler would do anything to make sure I'm happy. He would move mountains if it meant giving me something that I want. How can I not love someone like that?

The rest of the day passes in a series of beautiful scenes filled with happiness and laughter. Endless food and alcohol are consumed; music fills the air as our guests dance and mingle. It's been prepared to be the wedding to end all weddings as two prominent families are united through our love for each other. Everything is as it should be, everything is right with the world, and I'm afraid I might burst because I'm so full of joy right now.

"The moment I saw you in that first class, I knew I was going to marry you," he tells me. My arms wrap around Tyler's neck as we sway back and forth to the beautiful ballad.

I laugh and shake my head at him. "Confident, huh?"

He always says he knew...well, hoped, from the minute I walked into my Econ class that he and I would be together. I, on the other hand, wasn't so sure. I'd had a crush on someone else, but it didn't take long for me to reciprocate. Something about Tyler got to me. It was more than his looks, although his dark brown eyes and killer smile didn't hurt. He had a level of confidence unlike anyone I'd ever met before. It poured out of him, making him almost infectious to be around. Getting to know him and spending time with him became almost necessary to me.

I remember being the envy of every girl in that class when he and I were paired off together to do our semester project. We spent a lot of time together studying and researching during that time and every day we grew closer and closer until I finally realized I had fallen in love with him. That's all it took for us to become inseparable, for us to become Tyler and Everly, and now look at us—married and about to start a life together.

I place a chaste kiss on his lips. "You know, if I could have created my dream man from scratch, he would have been you. I know now that you were meant for me."

"Mmm, baby, I'm going to take you out of here in a few minutes and show you exactly why you'll never regret getting mixed up with a guy like me."

I lean into him and resting my head on his shoulder, letting out a sigh.

"I could never regret you, Tyler; you're the love of my life."

"And you're mine," he replies, placing a kiss on the top of my head.

We wanted to make sure to thank every last person who came to celebrate our day with us, so we stayed at the reception till the end. It's after midnight when Tyler and I stumble our way back into our room for the night after the last guests have left the banquet hall located inside the hotel. It's a gorgeous beachfront hotel, the ideal location for a wedding and convenient because many of our guests decided to spend the night here, too. I stand in the middle of the dimly lit room in my stunning ivory wedding gown, fitted at the top making it almost skintight, and then flaring at the bottom in a mermaid style. The back is see-through with a seam of tiny pearl buttons running up my spine. The details and appliqués are stunning and hand sewn, making it a one of a kind dress. Anticipation courses throughout my body as Tyler pours two glasses of champagne and hands me one.

"To my beautiful bride and the beginning of our life together. I can't wait to spend forever with you."

"To forever," I toast in agreement.

I take a long sip from my flute before placing it on the small table. I step back slowly, watching Tyler take a drink, his eyes never leaving mine. I reach around my back and release the first of many buttons that hold my dress together.

"Let me," he whispers, putting his glass down and making it across the room in two strides. He circles me until he's behind me and slowly begins to take out the pins of my hair, releasing my elaborate up do. Once he's satisfied that he has them all, he uses his fingers to shake out my hair until it falls in soft waves, framing my face.

I sigh as he kisses my bare shoulder, making my body shiver with excitement. His fingers lightly travel up to my ear where he removes my earring then gently tugs on my earlobe with his teeth. This earns a gasp of shock from me, and I've barely recovered before he removes the other earring.

My body grows warmer with Tyler leaving a trail of kisses down my neck, shoulders, and finally the top of my dress. I feel his powerful hands begin to undo the buttons, my dress getting looser as he opens each one.

"Hands up over your head, wife," he teases softly. Giving me a command is very unlike Tyler. He's more about asking me what I want, letting me tell him what will make me feel good which is nice...but I really like this.

Hearing him call me his wife is strange, but it's strange in the most incredible way. In the way that makes me believe that dreams do come true because from the moment I allowed myself to fall in love with him, Tyler West has been my biggest dream. *To forever*, I think to myself as he continues his sweet seduction.

I lift up my arms for him as he bends down and gathers the hem of my dress in his hands. He effortlessly lifts it up over my head, tossing it on a nearby chair. His hooded gaze scours the entire length of my body, taking in my bare breasts and the flimsy strip of ivory material I was assured were panties. I can see the exact moment when his eyes pool with desire; it's the same moment my desire pools between my thighs. The look in his eyes is almost too much.

"Jesus, Everly, you take my breath away."

I say nothing in return, just stare at him trying my best to memorize his face, memorize how he is looking at me right now. I don't know why I do it—but it feels like it's important, like I should never forget how he looks at this moment. I didn't think it would ever be possible to love him as much as I do or love him more than I did when I woke up this morning, but right now, I think I just might. It's the most beautiful and scary feeling in the world to put yourself out there like that, give your heart away so effortlessly to another person.

"Sit down on the bed," he demands in a husky voice laced with desire.

I do as he asks, backing up until the back of my legs hit the edge of the mattress. I lower myself down until I'm sitting and facing him. He reaches for his glass and gulps down the rest of his champagne before striding across the room and bending down before me. He reaches down and grabs hold of my ankle; he releases the strap and slides my bejeweled shoe off my foot. Once he's divested me of both shoes, I reach down and begin to unbutton his shirt while he undoes his cufflinks.

I waste no time in shoving the shirt off his shoulders while he helps me slide it off. Tyler gets to his feet, pulls his undershirt over his head, and starts to remove his pants.

"Slide back and lie down for me, baby." His voice is even hotter than before, he's taking control in a way that I'm not used to, and it's only getting me more excited. His words make me even wetter, needier for him; he's never been like this before. I do as I'm told while he takes care of the rest of his clothing; I shudder as I take in the sight of him in all his glory. Tyler. My husband. Mine. For as long as we both shall live. He's my life now, my world, and I intend to make him as happy as he makes me.

He climbs onto the bed, crawling up until he's hovering over me, and we're face to face. His eyes burn into me, filling me with a heady combination of love and lust.

"Have I mentioned how beautiful you are?"

I let out a sigh and smile shyly. "So are you."

"I love you, Everly. I fucking love you so much. I promise you that no matter what, no matter what happens, I'll always take care of you."

"Make love to me, husband," I whisper, keeping the tears at bay. No wife has ever felt this happy because there's only one Tyler, and he's all mine.

To forever...

The shrill sound of a nearby telephone wakes me. I open my eyes and try to get my bearings. It takes me a second to realize that I'm at the hotel. I peek over my shoulder, and Tyler is still sound asleep. Who could possibly sleep through that ringing?

I reach over to the nightstand and grab the receiver, bringing it up to my ear.

"Hello?"

"This is your courtesy wake-up call," says the voice on the other line.

"Thank you," I reply before hanging up. I throw my head back on the pillow and stretch my arms up over my head.

"Ty, we have a flight to catch, babe," I groan out mid-stretch. Excitement starts to build at the thought of Tyler and me on a beach, sipping drinks and soaking each other up.

I roll my head to the side and smile at the sight of my sleeping husband. My husband... I still can't believe that we're married.

"Come on, Ty. We have to start getting ready."

He turns his head to squint at me. "It's still early, babe. Our flight isn't until later."

"I know, honey, but by the time we get up, get ready, and have breakfast, it'll be time to go.

9

The airport is over an hour away. Did you take into account travel time?"

I hear a low chuckle escape from his lips. "All right, go hop in the shower. I'll be up by the time you're done."

I smile at him. Tyler has never been a morning person and getting him out of bed is always a challenge, but he's right, we have time. "Okay. But you better be up by the time I come back in here," I say. I place a quick kiss on his lips and make my way to the bathroom. I take a few minutes inspecting my reflection in the mirror, funny... I know it's silly, but I thought I'd look different as if getting married changes you somehow.

I take my time in the shower, enjoying the feel of the warm water on me. I imagine that Tyler is probably still in bed, and I think about the things we could do together if I just went back into the room and crawled in beside him. Tyler knows me like the back of his hand; he knows exactly what to do to set me off and with him, it's always sweet. From the beginning, it's always been about making love, expressing how we feel about each other intimately. I don't know if it can get any better than that. Although, it was a nice change when he was a little bossy in bed yesterday—that might be fun to explore in the future. I turn off the shower and dry myself before wrapping the oversized towel around my body. I towel dry my hair and run a brush through it before exiting the bathroom. As I walk back into the bedroom, I notice that Tyler is up and dressed already.

"You're actually up already?" I question with amazement. "Aren't you going to take a shower?"

He walks over to me wrapping his arms around my waist and pulling me in for an embrace. "I'll grab a shower when I get back, babe. Luca dropped by and asked me to give him a ride home. He spent the night at the hotel, too, and apparently his date ditched him last night."

I make no attempt to hide my annoyance when I use my hands to push at his chest enabling me to disengage from him. "You're joking, right?" It comes out as more of a warning than a question.

"No," he sighs. "It'll take me a half hour tops, babe. He's my best friend; what do you expect me to do?"

"How about telling him to call a cab?"

"Is that what you'd do if Morgan knocked on the door right now?"

He has me there; I'd never deny my best friend anything, but Luca is different. He's always been a source of contention in my relationship with Tyler. He and I have never gotten along, and I hate the fact that he has the power to cause tension between Ty and me.

"All right, fine. Go. You always come to the rescue where he's concerned." Arguments like these are not uncommon for us, but the day after our wedding, when we're about to go on our honeymoon... Even I can't believe this shit.

"Please don't be that way. He's like a brother to me," he says reaching out and grabbing my hand. "But you...you are my wife, and we're about to leave on our honeymoon and have an amazing time. It'll be just you and me." He pulls me closer, wrapping his arms around my waist and placing a kiss on my neck. "And when we get to Antigua, Ev... I'm not letting you out of the room for at least twenty-four hours... At least!" he declares with a twinkle of mischief in his eyes.

"You promise?"

"Mmm hmm."

11

I let out a sigh; he knows he's won me over already.

"Get yourself dressed and ready, and I'll be back before you know it. I'll take you to breakfast on the way to the airport."

"All right, but hurry up."

"I will." He releases me and grabs his keys off the nightstand. "I love you," he calls out right before he reaches the door.

"I love you, too," I say with a sigh. He stops and looks at me, his hand resting on the doorknob; he looks torn.

"You're really upset about this, aren't you?"

"It's just that this is our time. It's supposed to be about us, and I thought maybe just for once, you could forget about your loyalty to Luca. Just once."

"Shit, babe, I didn't know you felt like this." He closes the distance between us pulling me into an embrace. I melt into him, needing him to choose me, to choose us. I don't know why it's so important to me, but it feels crucial.

"I've been trying to tell you, but you just don't hear me."

"All right." He pulls away slightly, lowering his lips to my forehead. "You're right, this is just about you and me. I'll go let Luca know I can't take him, okay?"

"Really?" I question releasing a sigh of relief.

"Yes, really. I'll be back in five minutes, and I'll be ready to leave for the airport within the hour, okay?"

"Thank you."

"You're welcome, wife."

⸻

Something is off...I can feel it. Ty and I made it to the airport with time to spare and even though he chose to be here with me over helping Luca, I can tell that he's on edge.

"Are you all right?"

"Hmm? Yeah, I'm fine, babe. I just hate flying, it makes me anxious."

I guess that makes sense; I've never been much of a great flyer myself. In fact, I look outside of the window of the airport gate we're waiting in and begin to get restless at the size of the massive planes out there. To make matters worse, maintenance issues have delayed our plane so who knows how long we'll actually be stuck here. Tyler's glancing down at his cell phone every few minutes, bouncing his leg up and down and trying to rid himself of the nervous energy.

"You want me to get you a coffee or something?" I question, trying to get his mind off our flight.

He smiles at me, leans over, and places a kiss on my forehead. "Coffee would be great, babe. Thanks."

I walk over to the little coffee–book shop adjacent to the gate and order two coffees. I pick up a copy of the latest entertainment tabloid to read while I wait and pick up a paperback of a new law thriller for Tyler.

"Thought you might like this." He takes the book and the cup of coffee from my hands and smiles.

"This is supposed to be a great book. Thanks."

I take a sip of my coffee and sit down next to him. "You're welcome."

Tyler slips an arm around my shoulders and pulls me into his side allowing me to relax into him. My head drops to his shoulder, and he places a kiss on the top of my head. I listen to the announcements overhead, hoping that our flight is announced soon when Ty's phone rings.

"Hello?" he answers without even looking at the caller ID. It's almost as if he was expecting

13

the call. "Hold on, hold on, slow down." He shoots up out of his seat and steps away from the chairs to stand over by the windows. I follow him with my gaze, growing frightened by the look on his face. "Holy shit, is he all right?"

Something is obviously very wrong; I push off from my chair and walk over to where Ty's standing. I come up behind him and place my hand on his shoulder. He turns to face me, and I give him a questioning look.

"All right, we're on our way. Call me if you hear anything else." A chill runs down my spine, and my body freezes in fear.

"What's going on?"

"Luca was shot, we have to go."

"What? Oh, my God, what happened?"

He grabs my hand and stops at the chairs only to pick up our carry-on luggage before he's hauling me out of the airport. I practically have to run to keep up with him. I'm trying to make sense of what happened. I don't understand how this could even be possible. Luca has never been my favorite person or maybe it's the other way around, but I would never wish for him to end up hurt like this. Our bags land in the backseat with a thump, and we jump into Tyler's car. He's out of the parking lot faster than I'm comfortable with. I brace myself as he speeds toward the expressway trying to make a dent in the forty-five minute drive.

"Ty, what happened?"

"I don't know. It looks like a carjacking." His nerves are shot, I can tell. Tyler and Luca are like brothers, thick as thieves. If something were to happen to him, it would destroy Tyler.

"Who called you?"

"His mom."

"Did she say he was going to be all right?"

"I don't know." He answers in a short tone. I know he's upset, and my questions are probably just making things worse, so I back off.

"We'll reschedule the honeymoon for as soon as we can, all right? I just can't leave knowing my best friend was just shot."

"Tyler, I don't care about that. Of course, we should go to the hospital. Don't worry about me."

His knuckles begin to change color as he grips the steering wheel harder. I feel for him—he's obviously scared. I know I'd feel the same thing if something ever happened to my best friend, Morgan. She's the closest thing I have to a sister, too. Fear grips my heart, and I silently begin to pray that Luca will be all right for his sake as well as Tyler's.

We make it to the hospital in no time at all. Tyler is out of the car and running as soon as he shifts the car into park. I'm thankful that I wore sneakers today as I break off into a sprint behind him. By the time I catch up, he's at the front desk getting information. He grabs my hand and tugs me down a long corridor.

"He's still in surgery," are the only words he says to me as he pulls me on the elevator. I get a strange feeling of déjà vu; it's almost like I've been here before, like I've felt this fear before. I quickly shake the feeling off, push the fear aside, and steel my spine. Tyler needs me, and I need to be strong for him just the way I'd expect him to be for me if the roles were reversed.

As soon as we get off the elevator, we practically run into Kathy and Ted Jenson, Luca's parents.

"Tyler, Everly. I'm so glad you're here," Kathy says, grabbing Tyler's hand and giving it a pat.

"What happened exactly?"

"All we know is that he was shot in his car at the park."

I shake my head. "What was he doing at the park."

"We're not sure." I turn toward Ted, who's putting his arm around his wife now. God, I feel so terrible for them. The thought of your only son being shot in broad daylight is unimaginable.

"What are the doctors saying?" Tyler asks, his brows furrow as he's unable to hide his anxiety.

Kathy lets out a sigh; she looks exhausted, as though the weight of the world is on her shoulders at the moment. "The nurse came out earlier. She said that he was shot twice, once in the leg and once in the chest. He was critical but still breathing. Assuming that the bullets didn't hit any major arteries, they're hoping for the best."

I take hold of her hand, hoping to reassure her. "He's going to be fine."

She nods her head and wipes away her tears with her free hand. My heart breaks for her and what she must be going through. I'd imagine that this would be any parents' worst nightmare—the prospect of losing a child.

"Luca Jenson?" We all turn simultaneously with bated breath. The doctor stands there looking detached, and I can't read his features, he's showing no emotions. I wonder if that's part of their training in med school. We walk over to him as a group because there's strength in numbers and we're hoping that all of our positive energy will bring us good news.

Ted steps forward. "We're his family."

All of a sudden, I feel out of place, like I don't belong amongst this group of people who love this man. Luca and I are not close, we never have been, and we never will be. I met him at the bookstore freshman year of college. Luca helped me with my books and was really great to me. He made a great first impression, but the next time I saw him was after Tyler and I had started dating. After that, he was always cold, dismissive, and at times, downright rude. Of course, I was just as rude to him because I couldn't let him walk all over me. So, in a nutshell, Luca and I are not besties. We are NOT family.

"He made it through surgery. We were able to remove the bullets, but he lost a lot of blood. He should be just fine. He's going to need physical therapy for his leg and time to recover."

Tyler gives my hand a squeeze. "Can we see him?"

"He's being taken to the ICU as soon as he's settled. You can go in one at a time."

Tyler seems a little calmer once the doctor has left. I think we're all just so relieved that Luca made it out of surgery—that has to be a good sign. If there's one thing I know about him, it's that he's a real pain in the ass. There's no way he's going to let a few bullets get in the way of him living his life. For the first time since I heard the news, I'm absolutely confident that he's going to be all right, and strangely enough, I get a feeling of peace knowing that Luca's still in the land of the living.

"Everly," I hear someone call out from a distance. "Everly, wake up." The soft graze of someone's hand on my arm wakes me up. I must have dozed off in the waiting room while everyone spent time visiting Luca. I focus my vision on Kathy, who's standing above me with a smile on her face.

"Is everything all right?"

"Everything is fine, Luca's awake and Tyler went to the cafeteria to get food for everyone. I thought you might like to go in and visit with Luca."

"Oh, I'm not sure if that's a good idea."

"Why not? I'm sure he'd love to see you. The more love we give him right now, the better." I hesitate not wanting to explain to her how much her son and I dislike each other. "Go on, you don't have to be afraid. He looks better already."

"Ahh, okay," I agree pushing up from my chair. How can I say no to her? She's had what's probably been the worst day of her life, and I don't want to upset her. Besides, I'm curious to see for myself how Luca's doing. I take the elevator up the two floors to the ICU and the nurses at the nurse's station direct me to his room. When I walk in, Luca's asleep. He's bandaged up and looks pale but otherwise not terrible; he actually looks peaceful in sleep. The machines that he's connected to and the wires running all over his body are frightening, to say the least. I've never seen someone hooked up to so much shit. It makes me feel like they could go off at any second and all hell would break loose.

"Don't just stand there, Ev. You can come in." I'm startled when he speaks; I must have been so focused on the machines that I didn't notice he had woken up.

"I'm sorry, I just didn't want to wake you," I tell him, walking further into the room and lowering myself onto the chair by his bedside. "How are you feeling?"

"Like I just got shot."

"Well, I'm glad that you're okay."

"Are you? I'd have thought if anyone wished me dead, it would be you."

"I don't want you dead, dummy. I just want you to not be an asshole all the time."

"Hey, what's with all the name calling?"

"I'm sorry; all these machines are freaking me out. I can leave if you want; I know I'm not exactly your favorite person."

"You're not my least favorite person, either. I actually don't mind the company."

"Okay, any word on how long you'll be here?"

"No, but I'm assuming it'll be a few days," he replies.

"How did this happen, Luca?" I question, curiosity getting the best of me.

"I thought I'd go to the park for a run. I was just at the wrong place at the wrong time, I guess."

Something about this seems off to me; I never knew Luca was a runner and why would he choose the morning after my wedding to go for a

19

run when he was likely hung over? I don't comment because, really, it's none of my business.

"Have the police been by?"

"They came by to take my statement a little while ago."

"Well, did they at least catch the person that did this?"

He takes a breath, and there's an unmistakable look of concern on his face. "Not yet."

"Well, I'm sure they'll get him soon." I give him a weak smile; I'm trying to reassure him, but the truth is they may never catch the guy— it's just the way of the world.

"Yeah, Everly, just be careful out there. Watch your back, okay?" The undercurrent of his tone is all warning—a warning that sends chills down my spine.

"What's that supposed to mean?"

"Nothing, nothing. I'm sorry, it's just that I'm on edge. I'm just saying that if this could happen to me, it could happen to anyone. Maybe if I had been paying better attention, I could have avoided it."

His words make sense. I can see why he would feel that way, and I appreciate him taking the time to give me a warning.

"Luca Jensen, if I didn't know any better, I'd almost think that you cared about my well being."

"I do care, Everly. I know I'm an ass, but you're my best friend's wife, and that makes you family. I care."

"I don't know if I can handle you being nice to me. It's like I'm having an out of body experience or something."

"Ha. Don't make me laugh, it hurts."

"Sorry."

"What do you say we call a truce, Ev? Almost dying makes you see life a little differently. I don't want to waste my time fighting with you. Frankly, it's gotten a little out of control, don't you think?"

"I think I can agree to a truce."

"Good."

"I should get back out there. I'm sure your mom is dying to come back in here. Is there anything I can get you before I go?"

"No, but thank you for coming, it uh-it means a lot."

"You're welcome."

I leave the room feeling somewhat lighter, relieved that Luca is alive and on the road to recovery. I'm hopeful that he and I can move past our normally damaged relationship and become friends. Back in the waiting room, Tyler is on the phone in what seems to be a heated conversation. He doesn't look happy, and I try to move closer to him, but when he spots me, he holds up a finger letting me know that I should give him a minute, walking out of the waiting room. This isn't something new; Tyler is always on *important* phone calls though it's normally Luca who's calling to pull him away. I'm curious as to who he's talking to, but I respect his privacy so I let it go.

It's been almost a week since Tyler and I were married, a week since Luca was shot. It hasn't been easy with Luca hurt. We've been back and forth from the hospital daily. Tyler's taken it really hard. I've even heard him mumbling that it's all his fault as if he could have done anything to stop a random shooting. His moods have been unpredictable going from warm to cold, happy to mad, in the blink of an eye. Now that Luca is finally being released from the hospital, I'm hoping that Tyler will go back to his normal self.

Luca's parents are already there and engaged in a conversation when we walk into the waiting room today.

"He's going to need help getting around, Kathy. He needs someone to take him to physical therapy. The doctor's already told us that he shouldn't go home alone."

"Well, of course, he'll come home with us. It's just that with us both working full time, I don't know how much help we're really going to be able to give him."

"We'll have to look into hiring a nurse," Ted replies. They both look so stressed out, so tired, and I feel for them. All the extra care is likely to be a strain on their resources, and I can tell it weighs heavily on their minds.

"That's not necessary," Tyler says, putting his arm around me and pulling me close. "He can come stay with Everly and me. We have plenty of room in the new house, and I work at my father's law firm most days, but Everly's home. School doesn't start for another month and a half so one of us can always be with him."

There's no way that I can be hearing him correctly. There's no way that he would make a decision like this without consulting with me first. I can't believe he just volunteered me to practically take care of Luca around the clock. Yes, we've called a truce but spending all of my free time with him is a bit much.

"Oh Tyler, we couldn't possibly impose on you. You're newlyweds. It's bad enough that you didn't get to go on your honeymoon."

I hate that I've been put on the spot like this, but it is in my power to help out, and the Jensen's have been through enough already.

They need help, and even though Tyler pushed me into it, I'm going to do it.

"It's no trouble, Mrs. Jensen. Tyler's right; we have the space and the time to help him.

"It's just a lot to ask, Everly."

I take her hand in mine and give it a squeeze. She needs my reassurance, and I want to give it to her. As much as I hate the idea of taking this on, I'll do it for Kathy, who deserves to let go of all of this stress. And I'll do it for Tyler, who for some reason is carrying a guilt around that I'll never quite understand. And I guess I'll do it for Luca, too, in the spirit of our newly formed truce. "But you're not asking. We're offering."

"You're sure it's no trouble?"

"I'm positive. It's really not and you can come see him any time you want."

Tyler releases his hold on me but places a kiss on my forehead. "I'm going to go tell Luca the plan and make sure he's cool with this."

I take in the look of relief on Kathy's face, and I feel good about it. I'm happy that we're able to take this off her shoulders. I can deal with a bit of inconvenience if it means that she can rest a little bit easier. I just hope that Luca and I can really manage to put the past behind us and move on, I always thought he and I should have been friends. I never really understood why he disliked me so much to begin with.

Luca seemed on edge during the drive home from the hospital. I caught him glancing around the street while the car was stopped at traffic lights, almost as if he was waiting for the gunman to come back and finish the job. His relief was evident once we made it back to the house, I guess I'd be a little paranoid, too, if I'd

23

have just gotten shot and the person who did it was still on the loose.

What's strange is that Tyler looked equally paranoid; I caught him looking in the rearview mirror more times than I can count, way more times than necessary. Something is going on that I can't put my finger on. I've noticed what seems to be a rift between Luca and Tyler, although they'd probably deny it, but I can see it. I can tell something is off. Tyler just brushes me off when I ask him about it, telling me that I'm imagining things and everything is fine. But he's been harsher with me the last few days, too. He's short with me, gives me curt responses to questions I ask, and it's beginning to piss me off. What's worse is that we haven't had sex since our wedding night. I know it's only been about a week, but in all the time we've been together, I don't think we've ever gone that long. The few times I tried to initiate something, he told me that he was tired or had a headache. He has me beginning to wonder if I've done something wrong, something to push him away.

Once we get home, Luca allows Tyler to help him to the couch while I go upstairs and set up one of the spare bedrooms for him. I put the bag that Kathy packed for him on the chair and lay out fresh sheets on the bed. I picked the only other bedroom that connects to a bathroom so that he doesn't have to go far.

I find Luca lying on the couch, television remote in hand, flipping through the channels when I head back downstairs. He looks up when he hears me and gives me an almost shy smile.

"Where's Ty?" I question, picking up an old knitted blanket that's thrown over a chair.

"He went to pick up my pain meds and a few other things I need from home."

"Here you go," I say covering his bottom half with the blanket.

"Thanks."

"This is weird, huh?"

"Little bit. I never imagined being disabled and at your mercy."

This makes me laugh. "You know, I could really make you pay for being such a jerk all these years."

"But then you'd be breaking the truce. Are you prepared to do that because I will recover eventually, and I might just make you pay, Ev."

His threat sends an unexpected jolt of heat surging through me. I know he didn't mean that to be sexual in nature, but holy shit, my body took it that way and I don't understand its reaction.

"Relax," I say, my brain urging my body to recover from its betrayal. "The truce remains intact."

"Good because I really do want us to be friends. There's really no reason we shouldn't have been all along."

"Why weren't we?"

"I don't know, Ev. I was just immature."

I don't push further, even though I feel like there's more to it than he's saying. There must be a reason for his reaction toward me all this time. As for me, I couldn't help but to resent him because of his constant presence in Tyler's life, for the countless time he would call for a favor or a problem and Tyler would leave me to go help him. There were times when I thought that he was doing it on purpose, finding excuses to summon Ty because he knew it pissed me right the fuck off. Maybe this truce we've formed will finally put an end to all of it. Maybe Luca and I can finally be civil around one another, finally be friends.

25

"I'm going to make some lunch, you hungry?"

"I could eat."

"How about a sandwich?"

"Sounds great," he says, settling back into the couch. I head into the kitchen to make lunch, and I spend the entire time thinking about his earlier threat and why I reacted the way I did. I love my husband, which makes my reaction even more disturbing to me. If I'm being honest, when I first met Luca at the student bookstore, before I met Tyler, I had liked him instantly. In those first few moments, I had hoped that he'd ask me out, but he didn't, and when I met Tyler, I let go of that hope.

"That was a third of the money. The message you sent was uncalled for." I stand in the kitchen, making my morning cup of coffee with my ear to the open window listening to Tyler on a phone call.

"I need more time...No. No. I need at least a week." He sighs at whatever the person on the other line says. He's obviously agitated; I can hear it in his tone. I peek out the window and spy him pacing back and forth. He runs a hand through his hair looking very worried. "Yeah, I'll be in touch," he says before hanging up.

"What was all that talk about money?" I probe when he comes inside. He looks up at me, face guarded, and I swear I could feel an invisible wall going up. "I wasn't eavesdropping, Ty," I say in my defense. "The window is open, and you weren't exactly whispering."

He relaxes his shoulders. "I'm working a case with my dad. I was speaking to opposing council about a settlement."

"Oh. Okay." I feel relieved that it was something work related.

"Where's Luca?"

"Getting ready; he's got his first physical therapy session today. I'm driving him."

"Right. I'll pass on breakfast; I have to get to the office."

"Is everything okay between you and Luca? You've barely said two words to each other since he got out of the hospital."

"We're fine. I'm just busy, and he's had a traumatic experience. I'm just giving him time to heal. It's not like we can go shoot the shit, Everly."

I nod, not satisfied with his answer but deciding to let it go. He's too much on edge to get any information out of him now. I'll have to try again another time. Something is wrong, I can tell. Tyler and Luca are inseparable, always have been, and over the last few days the tension between them has been obvious, and I feel like a spectator that started watching just a little too late. With a quick kiss goodbye, Tyler leaves and I prepare two travel mugs of coffee.

"Ty gone?"

I look up; my gaze lands on Luca standing in the doorway leaning on a cane and my stomach flutters. My first thought is that even disabled, he looks hot—and I have no idea where it came from or why all of a sudden I can't control what I feel and think about him.

"Yeah, he just left. Are you ready to go?"

"Ready as I'll ever be."

I give him a half smile and nod. I know this can't be easy for him, when the bullet hit his leg, it tore through tendons making physical therapy necessary. I'm sure it can't be fun, but the doctors say that with about six weeks of therapy, his leg should be good as new.

"Made you a cup of coffee to go." I dangle the travel mug in the air like a prize.

"Just what I need." He grins. "Thanks."

"You're welcome," I say, grabbing my purse and my car keys off the kitchen island.

"Let's do this." When I reach Luca, I grab hold of his arm wanting to help him out of the house and into the car. He looks down at my hand on him and something passes his features, I'm just not sure what. He levels his eyes on mine.

"It's okay, Ev. I've got it."

My cheeks heat with a twinge of embarrassment. "Sorry, I was just trying to help."

"I know; it's okay."

"Can I at least open the car door for you?"

"Sure, Ev." He chuckles. I kind of like when he calls me Ev, not many people do, Tyler certainly never does. He hops (literally hops) in the car, and I shut the door behind him as he settles the cane against his seat.

I pull out of the driveway and head out in the direction of the clinic.

"Thanks for doing this. I know it's not easy having someone you can barely stand in your life and having to take care of them. I know you gave up a lot to be here, your honeymoon, your privacy."

"It's okay."

"No, it's not. You should have never been dragged into this; it's not cool."

"It's fine, Luca. It's not like any of this is your fault."

I look over at him and something flashes in his eyes. He looks angry for a moment but quickly masks his features.

"I know it's not my fault but still...You're really helping me out and taking the pressure off my parents, and I appreciate it."

"I'm glad to do it," I assure him with a smile. A truce with Luca is not something that I could ever foresee happening, but now that it has, I kind of like it. This is how I pictured things between us all those years ago when we first

29

met. It's how things should have been, but for some reason, we just couldn't get along. "Is this weird?"

"What?"

"This truce of ours?"

"It's a little weird, but mostly it's just nice."

"I keep waiting for you to say something rude."

He chuckles and shakes his head. "I promise I'm not going to say anything rude."

We ride along for a while with nothing but the music from the stereo filling the car, and it's a comfortable silence

"Hey, Luca? Is there something going on with you and Tyler?"

"What do you mean?"

"You seem angry at him, and he seems like he's trying to avoid you at all costs."

"Listen, Everly..."

"If it's because he didn't take you home that day—don't blame him, Luca, please. It was my fault; I didn't want him to go, and he stayed behind because of me."

"Nothing that happened that day was your fault. Don't put that on yourself."

"Yeah, but if I would have just let him go..."

"This didn't happen because Tyler didn't take me home. I made the choice to go to the park, and it has nothing to do with you."

Something about this conversation seems wrong, like things happened that shouldn't have happened. It's like I'm missing a key part of the story, and I can't figure out what it is. It's like a secret locked away in a book somewhere left for me to find. I hang out in the waiting room while Luca does his physical therapy, my brain still going in circles trying to figure out exactly what it is that's going on. The answer is right there, I can feel it just below the surface waiting for me to discover it. I let it go before it begins to drive me crazy and I let my mind drift off to all of the other things I have to do, like get ready for law school even though I'm not so sure I really want to go. I think the fact that Tyler wanted to be a lawyer motivated me to do the same, but I don't think I have the drive for it that he has. I know I'd be good at it, though, and for now, that's enough for me.

It's been two weeks since Luca was released from the hospital and came to stay with us. Two weeks of Tyler avoiding Luca and barely speaking to me. He gets up, goes to work, comes home, and goes to sleep—that's the extent of his routine. I don't know what's gotten into him, and the more I ask, the further away he pushes me. What's worse is that all of the time I should be spending with my new husband, I've been spending with his best friend, instead.

I like it—it scares the hell out of me, it keeps me up at night, and I know that it's wrong. Every fiber of my being knows that it's wrong, but I still can't stop how I feel. I like every single minute that I've spent with Luca; I've come to cherish the time that we spend together because when I'm with him, it's only me—he only sees me. There are no emergency phone calls, no random text messages. There are no sporting events that take precedent, no one from work pulling him away. It's just me, and I love it.

"You want another slice of pizza?" I ask Luca.

"Don't try to distract me," he says, lining up the remote before taking a step toward the TV and swinging his arm forward. "Haha! Strike," he yells spinning around on his good leg and grinning at me. Who knew virtual bowling could be so much fun? Looking at him now, you could barely tell that he was shot just a few weeks ago.

"All right, show off, my turn," I chastise, picking up my remote and taking my place in front of the TV. I suck at bowling—I suck at it in real life, and I suck at it equally as bad in video games, so I'm not looking forward to yet another virtual gutter ball.

"Line up the shot, Ev, and when you release the ball twist the remote just a little bit."

"What's that going to do?"

"Just trust me," he says with a chuckle.

I look at him skeptically but follow his instructions anyway and knock down six pins. "Yay." I jump up excitedly.

"Nice job. Go again," he encourages.

I line up my shot; he comes up behind me, his hands on my waist, and pushes me slightly to the side. "This is where you should be."

His warm breath on the nape of my neck makes me shudder slightly. I hate how my heart rate speeds up because of his proximity, and yet, I love having him this close. I take the shot quickly and miss the remaining pins, but I don't care. I need to get some distance. I plop on the couch and pick up my cell phone to find an unread text message.

"I just got a text from Tyler," I say looking up at Luca.

His voice turns almost icy. "What's it say?"

"It says he's working late with his dad and he'll be home late again." He's been home late just about every single night over the last two weeks, and I honestly believe he's doing it so that he can avoid Luca.

"Hmm."

"What?" I glance up at him arching my brow in question. "What's the hmm for?"

"Nothing," he says turning his attention back to the video game. I'm up and out of my seat to snatch the remote before he can pull away.

"Are you going to tell me what's going on with you and Ty? What's the issue?"

He shrugs his shoulders at me. "There's no issue."

"Luca."

"I just think that he needs to get his priorities in order."

"Right because that's not cryptic at all."

"It's all I'm going to say for now."

"Why, why won't you tell me what's going on."

"What kind of man would leave his brand new wife to give a friend a ride home?"

I take a step back and look at him in confusion.

"What kind of friend would ask a guy that just got married to take him home?"

"Good question."

"Are you saying you didn't ask him? Is that what you're saying?"

"I'm not saying anything. You need to ask him, and you need to open your eyes," he says turning to walk away. But I'm not done with him, not done with this conversation. I follow him to the staircase and grab his arm just before he reaches the first step.

"Wait."

He turns back to me, and when he does, he snakes his arm around my waist, pulls me into him and lowers his lips to mine. His bold move takes me aback. I brace my hands on his shoulders out of pure shock, I think. I know I should use my position to push him away and tell him no, but instead, I do the unthinkable—I do the unspeakable—and I kiss him back. I part my lips in invitation, one that he accepts immediately as he slides his tongue into my

33

mouth. I push all logical thoughts out of my head and allow myself to feel, to take everything that he's giving me and enjoy every single second of it. In the end, Luca pulls away before I do. He looks down at me, his eyes full of lust, but his body language is taut, frigid, and full of remorse.

"I'm sorry Ev. I shouldn't have done that."

"I know. I'm sorry, too. I should have…"

"No, you didn't do anything wrong. It was me."

"It wasn't just you. It's been happening for a while now, hasn't it? I'm not the only one that feels it, am I?"

"No, you're not the only one, but it doesn't matter. You're married, and that's the bottom line."

"I know. You're right."

"I'm leaving in the morning."

"You don't have to do that. It was one mistake."

"It was one hell of a mistake, and if it happens again, I can promise you that I won't be the one pulling away."

"But—"

"I'm all right. I'm recovered enough to be on my own again, and it's time to get back to real life. I'm moving to Chicago at the end of the summer anyway. You know that I'm going to law school there. You won't have to see me."

"You're my friend, Luca, it's not like that. We've moved passed hating each other."

"Yeah, maybe we did a little too good of a job with moving forward," he says before walking up the stairs.

He's right; it was a mistake, a huge fuck up on both of our parts. I never thought I'd be the kind of girl who would do something like this, the kind of girl who would cheat on her husband. But for the last few weeks, my husband has been gone in every way that matters, and in that time, Luca has crept into a place in my heart. *Holy shit,* I can't believe I just had that thought. I can't believe that this is happening, and if it was so wrong then why the fuck does the knowledge that Luca is leaving tomorrow leave me feeling so sad?

4

The front door slams, alerting me that Tyler is home. I close my eyes preparing to tell him what happened between Luca and me earlier, until I hear loud voices from downstairs. I throw the covers off me and tread lightly into the hallway. I reach the stairs but stop myself from going downstairs when I hear Luca's voice.

"You're never going to learn, are you? Look at what happened to me, dude."

"Just stay out of it," is Tyler's response.

"Stay out of it? Stay the fuck out of it? Are you fucking kidding me right now? You put me right the fuck in it, Ty."

"I'm taking care of it."

"Yeah and what about Everly, huh?" I slide down against the wall and come to a sitting position; I'm not sure how I feel about Luca bringing me up right now.

"What about her?" Ty questions, sounding like he's being put out, like he has better things to do than to have this discussion with Luca.

"You abandoned her. You left her in this house for the last few weeks, and you're nowhere to be found."

"She hasn't been alone. She's had you around."

"You're right, she has had me, but what about the fact that I kissed your wife tonight, does that matter?" The silence is scary; I can only imagine what Tyler is thinking right now. The sound of something shattering startles me, but I stay put. I need to figure out what's happening with my husband.

"You did what?" Tyler shouts, his voice echoing throughout the whole house. I should be pissed at Luca for telling him before I could, but he was going to find out anyway. At least this way, I get to hear how he really feels.

"You heard me, asshole."

"Why, for revenge? Is that why you would do that to me?"

I'm waiting with bated breath to hear this answer; would Luca really have kissed me to make a point? To get back at Tyler for whatever it is he thinks that Tyler has done?

"No, you arrogant son of a bitch. I kissed her because, unlike you, I actually give a fuck about that girl up there."

"Oh my God, not this shit again. Please, it was FOUR years ago. She chose me."

"Really? Did you give her a choice? Does she know, did she ever know, how I felt about her?"

My breath hitches at Luca's revelation, did he want me back then? All those years ago when we met, could he have actually liked me? I thought that we had made a connection after our initial meeting but convinced myself I was wrong after he turned into a complete asshole when Tyler and I got together.

"It's not my fault that you didn't have the balls to tell her." Tyler's voice is full of venom; I've never heard him sound like that before.

"No, it's your fault that I never got the fucking chance!"

37

"She's my wife, Luca, whatever claim you think you had on her died the minute we got married. Stay the fuck away from her."

"I'll stay away, but the minute your bullshit touches her, I'm done." The front door slams, and I know Luca is gone. I quickly rush into the bedroom and hop into bed. Luca comes up a few minutes later; he slides into bed and lays down throwing his arm over his eyes.

"Is there something you need to tell me?" he probes.

After what I've heard, I'm not in the mood for games, not in the mood to beat around the bush or keep him in the dark the way he's done to me.

"I think you already know."

"That's just fucking great. My wife of less than a month kisses my best friend. That's fucking perfect."

"First of all, I didn't kiss him, he kissed me, and second, what do you care, you're never around anyway."

"You know what? I'm not doing this with you; I'm not having this conversation."

"Of course, you're not. That would actually require you to be present; it would require you to feel something."

"Goodnight, Everly," he says, shutting me out yet again, closing the door on all conversations. I want to cry, but I don't I won't allow myself to. It would be so easy for me to sit here and use tears as a way to get him to open up, but it's not a manipulation when it's real, when the sadness is real. I'm lonely in this bed and the loneliness is palpable, it's consuming, and I don't know how much more I can possibly take.

I close my eyes and force myself to go to sleep, force myself to push all of the questions, all of the doubt, all of the confusion out of my head at least for one night. I tell myself that I'll confront Tyler in the morning and force him to tell me the truth, but when I wake up, I'm alone again and Tyler is nowhere to be found.

⁂

Tyler's getting worse; it's been days since our argument, since the night Luca left. He's barely been home, I can't get through to him, and he hardly speaks to me. I've tried waiting up for him at night, texting and calling him throughout the day, but he's just shut me out, and I have no idea why he's doing this to me. I don't think I've ever felt so lonely in my whole life, and the loneliness is palpable. It hurts every single time he rejects me, and it confuses me, confuses me because, with every passing day, I grow more comfortable with Tyler's seclusion and more distracted with thoughts of Luca.

Something is happening to me and it's scaring the hell out of me. I never thought I'd be the type of woman who would even so much as think about looking at another man. I love my husband; I wouldn't have married him otherwise, right? But then why are thoughts of Luca infiltrating my mind? I think back to the first time I met Luca, and it brings a smile to my face.

It's the weekend before school starts—my freshman year of college, and I'm at the campus bookstore trying to find the textbooks I need for my classes. The place is packed; I thought it would be a brilliant idea to wait until the last minute to get my books. I figured I'd bypass the crowds, but I was wrong—it's a zoo. I'm standing on a line that literally wraps around the entire store.

39

I mentally kick myself for not having gotten my books weeks ago. There were no baskets available when I came in and now I'm fumbling and struggling to keep my books from falling. I'm startled when out of nowhere someone reaches out and snatches some of the books out of my hands. I turn my body toward the man standing behind me in line, ready to snap at him, but my voice catches in my throat. He's stunningly handsome and tall, at least a foot taller than me, his dark hair is the perfect contrast to his green eyes, and I'm mesmerized.

"You looked like you could use a little help," he says with a grin.

"Uh yeah, thanks. There were no more baskets available when I came in."

Fuck, he's sexy, and all of a sudden, I feel self-conscious but try to keep my composure around him.

"Why don't you put your stuff in my basket? I have plenty of room."

"Oh, no it's okay."

"No seriously, I insist."

I hesitate for a moment. "You're sure you don't mind?"

"Positive."

I place the remaining books in his basket and smile up at him, trying not to get lost in his beautiful face. God, he's perfect.

"Thanks," is all I manage to mutter.

"I'm Luca."

"Nice to meet you, I'm Everly."

"Everly. That's a beautiful name."

"Thanks," I reply softly as I tuck a loose strand of hair behind my ear.

I can't describe the reaction I'm having toward this guy, I've never reacted like this to anybody else. There's just something about him that draws me in.

"Are you a freshman?" I question trying to fill the nervous silence.
"Yeah, how 'bout you?"
"Yup. Just got to campus yesterday."
"Living in the dorms?" he asks.
"Yeah, it would be an hour for me to commute. I didn't want to have to do that every day; what about you?"
"I grew up around here, next town over. My buddy and I have an apartment just off campus."
"Cool," I reply, excited just to talk to this guy, to be in his presence, and we do talk. For the next twenty minutes or so, we talk about school, compare schedules, talk about what we both hope to major in, and in the end, I walk away from him feeling slightly disappointed by his lack of interest in me. I feel a little sad that he didn't ask me out like I'd hoped he would. He didn't ask me for my number or give me any indication that he was interested in any more than sharing a basket and a conversation.

There were a few times after that initial meeting that I found myself wishing I would have taken a chance and asked him for his number or even given him mine, but a few weeks later, I met Tyler and let all thoughts of Luca go. I had no idea that he and Tyler were best friends, I had no idea about how small the world really is, that I could end up dating the best friend of the guy that I initially liked. But when I found out, I remember being confused for a while. I was confused as to who I really liked, but after seeing how poorly Luca treated me and how disinterested he was in having anything to do with me, I let the confusion go and focused my attention on Ty.

Now as I stand outside of Luca's apartment having just rung the doorbell, I wonder if maybe

I didn't just settle for the guy who gave me attention instead of pushing for the one that I really wanted.

"Ev? What are you doing here?"

"You haven't been answering my texts," I say pushing past him in order to gain entrance to his tiny one-bedroom apartment. He shuts the door and moves into the living room, coming to stand directly in front of me.

"I know. I'm sorry, it's just that after what went down, I thought we could both use the space."

"I get that Luca," I say with a slow nod. "But you're all that I have right now. Tyler's nowhere to be found, my marriage is falling apart, and I can't tell anyone. I can't talk to anyone about this because they wouldn't understand." I hate how desperate I sound; I hate how dramatic of a turn my life had taken that now Luca is the person I confide in when it used to be Tyler.

"When was the last time he was home?" he questions motioning toward the couch. I take a seat and pick up one of the throw pillows, hugging it close to me for comfort.

"He comes home in the middle of the night and sneaks out before I wake up. It's like he woke up one morning and decided all of a sudden that he didn't want to be married."

"Don't say that." He takes a seat next to me. "Tyler loves you."

"Then why do I feel like I've already lost him?"

"You need to talk to him, make him give you the answers you're looking for. Only he can do that for you."

"You know, though, right?"

He says nothing but the look on his face tells me that I'm right. I let out a frustrated sigh in response.

"Is he having an affair, Luca? Is that why?"

"No, he's not having an affair, but I can tell you that he's in over his head."

"I know it's terrible, but I wish that he was; I wish that's all that was wrong because then I wouldn't feel so guilty about how I'm feeling about you," I say it before I can even think about the words; it's an admission I had no intention of making, but now that it's out, I feel strangely liberated. He places his hand on my cheek, and I lean into it, letting his touch fill me with warmth.

"I feel it, too. You know that, right? We just can't go there, Ev, not now. If anything does happen between us, it needs to be because you're coming to me free and clear. I can't betray Ty like that, and I don't think you want to, either."

"You're right, just- will you at least answer my texts from now on, will you at least give me that?"

"Yeah, Ev, I'll give you that."

I push off the couch and come to stand. He follows suit putting his hand on the small of my back and walking me to the door. We stand there for a moment his eyes on mine and a feeling of sadness washes over me. I don't want to go, the pull that he has on me is stronger than I ever could have imagined.

"I heard what you told Tyler, about you never telling me how you felt about me."

He nods and gives me a shrug of the shoulders. "It's not like it's a secret anymore, is it?"

"Why didn't you ever tell me?"

"He got to you first, nothing I could do at that point."

"Is that why you were so mean to me?"

He leans in and touches his forehead to mine; I fight the urge to wrap my arms around his

43

neck. "Being a jerk was easier than admitting what I really felt, or worse, letting anyone else see how I really felt."

"I should go."

He opens the door for me, and I give him a quick peck on the cheek before walking out. I don't look back because looking back would only make leaving that much harder.

"So, you have no more pain in your leg?"

"No, it's finally starting to feel back to normal."

I relax into my pillow while holding the cell phone between my ear and my shoulder. These nightly phone calls with Luca have gotten me through the last few weeks; they're the one thing that I look forward to every day, the only thing I can rely on.

"Any word from Tyler?"

"I haven't spoken to him since he told me he was going away to that conference with his dad. He sends texts every day, but other than that, no."

I have the sneaking suspicion that the conference is an excuse. I'm not sure that there even is a conference. It would be easy enough to find out, I could call Tyler's dad, but I'm not so sure I want to know. It's almost easier to live in denial.

"How do you feel about that?"

"Numb," I answer honestly. "I never knew how fast a relationship could deteriorate. One minute I'm getting married and I'm the happiest girl in the world, and the next minute, it's all falling apart."

I hear an audible sigh from his end of the line. "I don't want to make things worse for you, Ev."

"You're not, Luca. You're the only thing keeping me sane right now. If it wasn't for you, I would have lost it already."

"Are you afraid of losing him?"

I give his question some thought before I reply and what I say is like a revelation to me. "I think I'm afraid of not having him in my life anymore. He's been a huge part of my world for the last four years, and I think I'd miss him—a lot. I just don't know if that means I'm afraid of losing him as my husband. I think right now it wouldn't hurt me as much as I thought it would."

"Losing him doesn't matter, Everly. It's you who'll end up being found, but you have to make that choice, no one else can make it for you."

"I know."

"Goodnight, Ev."

"Goodnight, Luca."

I end the call and put the phone on my nightstand. I should try to get some sleep, but sleep has been elusive lately. There's too much going on in my life, too much weighing on my shoulders, for me to be able to sleep soundly. I get out of bed, walk over to Tyler's ever-growing book collection, and peruse the different titles before finally deciding on one. I pull it from the bookshelf and sit down on the bed, using the propped up pillows as a backrest. I open the book and turn to the first page, startled when a folded piece of paper falls out onto my lap. Gingerly, I pick it up and unfold the paper, I recognize the handwriting to be Tyler's, but all the air goes out of my lungs when I see that it's addressed to me. I close my eyes bracing myself for whatever it is I'm about to read. When I finally open my eyes, I'm ready to read whatever it is that's in this note.

Dear Everly,

If you ever find this letter, I hope that it's years after I'm gone. I hope that you're in a time and place where whatever wounds I've left behind have healed. I'm scared, babe. I have a real problem, and I just don't see a way out. I don't know if I can fix what I screwed up, and if that's the case, you need to know that I never intended to hurt you. I never thought I'd let things get this bad, this far, or get so caught up that I would lose sight of what was really important. I've done so many things, things that I never told you, things that I'm not proud of but you... You, Everly, are the only thing that's right in all of the things I've done.

There are times when I can barely stand to look at you, to see the love and hope on your face because all I feel is guilt. Guilt that I've made you promises that I'm afraid I may not be able to keep, fear that I may not even make it to our own wedding. To think I might not see your face one day is the hardest thing to take. If the unthinkable happens, if I don't make it out of this, I want you to go on. I want you to get married, have babies, and see the world. Don't give up; don't hold back because the honest to God truth is I never really deserved you anyway. I was like a thief in the night, taking what I wanted, even though I knew it shouldn't have been mine. I don't regret it, though; I'd do it all over again for you. The only thing I would change about our life together is me and what my ambition did to us. I hope you never read this

47

letter, I hope everything turns out all right, and I can destroy it. That we get the life we always wanted, but if I don't, I want you to know that even if you can no longer hear my voice, I'll be right beside you, and I'll smile from wherever I am when you get the life I always wanted for you to have. I hope that one day you can forgive me. I hope you know how much having you meant to me.

I love you,
Tyler

What is this? I read the letter over and over again trying to make sense of it all, trying to understand exactly what it is that he feels guilty for and why he ever thought he wouldn't make it to our wedding day. I feel so lost and stupid. Am I really that oblivious that I don't know what's going on with my own husband?

"Everly?" I jump slightly and let out a surprised scream. I look up and see Tyler standing in the doorway. I didn't know he'd be home; why would I when he barely speaks to me.

"You're back."

"Yeah, how have you been?" he questions, pushing off from the doorway and walking over to me. My heart hurts at the sight of him. The sense of loss I feel is overpowering because I know that things are bad, likely beyond repair, and what makes it worse is that, after all that's happened, I still have no idea why. I feel like I'm stuck in eternal darkness—no matter how hard I try, I can't claw my way out to the light, and Tyler is the one who's stuck me here.

I can see the exact moment when he realizes what I'm holding in my hands. His body stiffens, and his face grows pale.

"Do you want to explain this to me?" I don't recognize my own voice; it's filled with so much hurt and defeat. He takes a seat on the edge of the bed, and I see it. For the first time, I can actually see the pain living behind his eyes, the exhaustion and the fear. I want to help him through whatever this demon is that's taken him away from me, but I'm afraid that it's just too late because while he left me alone and abandoned me, someone else snuck into my heart.

"I have made a mess of my life, and I've-"

"You've what?"

"I have been gambling for a very long time, Everly. It started off small; I'd bet on a sporting event here or there, made a little bit of money, and over time, it got worse."

"How much worse?"

"Bad. I'm in a lot of trouble, and I owe a lot of money to some very dangerous people. I have been trying to fix it, but it's not working. I have been doing everything I can think of to dig out of it, but it's hard."

"Can't you make payments?"

"I have; I've given them money."

"How much did you give them?"

"I gave them all the money we got for the wedding."

"Oh, my God, that was over thirty thousand dollars." I whisper it because I can barely breathe, barely move. "What have you done? Did that even make a dent in the debt?"

"Not really."

Luca warned me that Tyler has a problem, but I didn't understand. He told me to be careful, but I didn't know what he meant and now—now it all makes sense. Suddenly, the blinders are off and everything becomes crystal

49

clear, and with that new clarity, all I can feel is anger and betrayal.

"You were never giving Luca a ride home the morning after our wedding, were you? You were going to pay those men."

"Luca wasn't even at the hotel; he had gone home right after the wedding."

"So, when I gave you a hard time about leaving, you what?" I gasp because I get it now; I understand why Luca is so fucking angry with Tyler. "You called your best friend and had him deliver that money. Because of you, he was shot, and because of you, he could have been killed."

He makes no excuses, the remorse on his face is evident, the solitary tear that escapes his eyes at one point in time would have reduced me to a love-struck fool, but now it makes no difference. His sorrow no longer moves me, no longer tugs at my heartstrings, because the anger is too strong.

"My God, you've been lying to me for years. For years, I've thought that Luca was the issue between us, but the whole time it was just you. It was this thing that you've kept between us."

"It just got out of control, babe. It was never supposed to be like this. I just... I wanted more for us. I wanted you to have the wedding of your dreams and the house of your dreams."

"Oh, do NOT put this on me. Don't you fucking dare. You wanted those things, too, and I would have waited. I would have worked and waited until we could afford them. I would have gotten married with our closest family and friends, Tyler. I didn't need the huge wedding. If you had just talked to me, I would have told you that. I never asked you to live beyond your means... never."

"I wanted the best for you."

"You're using me as a scapegoat. This has nothing to do with me."

"You're right."

"What are you going to do now?"

"I- I don't know Everly, okay I don't know."

"Well, I'm going to tell you what you're going to do."

"Babe."

"Don't. Babe. Me. Don't! You are going to go to your father and tell him what's happening. You're going to borrow the money from him to pay these people off and then you are going to put this house on the market and use the money to pay your father back."

"Really? Where are we going to live?"

"I'm going to live on my own. You'll have to figure out where you're going to live for yourself."

"What are you saying?"

"I'm saying that I'm leaving. I'm leaving you, and it's not because you have a problem because everybody has those. It's because you have lied to me and manipulated me from the moment we met. Everything that I believed in was a fucking lie, and I cannot stand to be around you, not even for one more second."

"I love you. I swear to you, that's not a lie."

"Your love is tainted, your love is stifling me because it's clouded with deceit. There's no way for me to pick out which parts of it are true or real so that makes it all false. It voids everything."

He shoots up off the bed looking both hurt and angry; I'd be willing to bet that his expression matches my own. "Just like that? One bad thing happens and just like that you're leaving me?"

I get up and move to the closet, gathering a pair of sweats and a t-shirt from the shelves, and quickly begin to dress. "You don't get it, and I honestly don't think you ever will. Bad things happen all the time; it's how you handle them, and you chose to lie, you did this not me."

I pull a pair of socks out of the dresser drawer and sit on the bed in order to slide them on as he watches me in horror.

"You have abandoned me; you promised to love and cherish me, but you've been nowhere to be found. You should have told me the truth, and we could have gotten through this together, but instead, you've been on this solo mission doing God knows what and I'm done. I'm so done," I tell him as I slide my sneakers on my feet.

"Everly, please, you're all I have left."

"And I'm not going to stay here like a sitting duck waiting for someone to come after me to get to you."

"I would never let that happen."

"Right, I think if you asked Luca, he would have a different opinion. I mean, he nearly died because of you."

"That's not fair."

"You haven't been fair to me, to us. You married me all the while knowing that you were in trouble, you wrote me a letter—a fucking letter in case someone *murdered you!* What did you think, that it would make me feel better to find a letter three or four years from now telling me that you were a fuck-up but you loved me?"

"I just wanted you to know how I felt."

"It's great that you can be honest in a letter, Ty. You should try being that way in real life. Call your father; if I don't see a for sale sign on the lawn of this house in the next two days, I will call him myself."

"Everly."

"I'll come back another time for my things." I turn to face him, looking at him makes my heart ache, but his mountain of lies are too much for me to overcome. I give him the faintest of pecks on the cheek as I tell him goodbye. A solitary tear runs down my face for the loss of what could have been so full of beauty, a dream that will never come true now. I leave him standing there and the guilt makes me falter just a step, but I fight against the urge to stay. I fight because I know somewhere deep inside that this chapter of my life has to come to an end. Staying here with him another night could quite literally kill me.

I get in my car and drive, replaying that scene in my head over and over again. I try to determine the exact moment when my entire marriage fell apart and how the fuck I could have been so blind. The warning signs were there from the start, but in my defense, I didn't know what to look for. I vaguely register the sound of my cell phone ringing; I peer down to see my best friend Morgan's name pop up on the screen. Tyler's probably called her, he probably thinks that I'm going to her house and I should, that would be the logical place for me to go, or to my parents' house but I'm not. I pull onto Luca's street. I didn't plan to come here. I honestly didn't even think about it, this is just where I ended up. It's ironic that the one person that I could barely stand to be around turned out to be the person who I've come to depend on the most.

I park and switch off the ignition, quickly angling out of the car and jogging up Luca's front steps before I change my mind. With a deep breath, I ring the doorbell, wait about ten seconds before ringing it again, and again, and for good measure, again. I see a light go on through the front window, and then I hear footfalls along with what I'm pretty sure are curse words. The door flies open and I'm met by Luca's angry glare but I can't focus on that—my eyes have traveled down to his bare chest. I assumed he had nice abs from the fit of his clothing, but I had no idea how perfect they really were. And the sexiest pair of pajama bottoms I've ever seen sit low on his hips. Jesus, why did he have to open up the door shirtless? By the time I make it back to his face, the anger is now replaced with concern.

"Everly, are you okay? What are you doing here?"

"Can I come in?"

"Of course." He shakes his head almost like he's coming out of a trance and opens the door wider so that I can pass through. "What's going on?"

I say nothing. Instead, I dig Tyler's letter out of my purse and hand it to him. He reads it, and I take a seat on the couch and watch him, watch as the gamut of emotions that I felt a little while ago are displayed on his face.

"Everly, I don't even know what to say to this." He takes a seat next to me handing the letter back. "Where'd you find that?"

"In one of his books. He came home tonight, Luca, and I confronted him. He told me everything, the betting on sporting events, the money, how he used that money to pay for the wedding and what we put into the house. He told me how he sent you to the park that day. Why did you go?"

"He's my best friend. I didn't exactly think he'd put me in a situation where I'd go and be shot. I thought I was just going to deliver the money for him and be done with it, but of course, they weren't happy with a partial payment and you know the rest."

"I left him tonight, Luca."

55

"You did what?"

"It's done, it's over, I can't be with him anymore. Everything that we had was built on nothing but his lies. I can't trust him."

"How did he take it?"

"Not well, but I can't live my life worrying about how Tyler feels because Tyler has never given a damn about how I feel. My feelings are an afterthought to him."

"What are you going to do Ev?"

"For now?" I hesitate but force myself to be brave. "I was hoping I could stay with you."

His lips tip up in a smile, and my heart flutters a bit. "You're not going to make this easy on me are you?"

"What do you mean?"

"You know how I feel about you."

Our eyes are locked, and the intensity I get from his warm my entire body, makes every thought, every concern, every hurt fade away and for just the briefest of time, I forget about the things that have bound me. I lean in wanting nothing more than to draw more of Luca's warmth, it radiates all around me as my lips touch his. It happens that fast, that abruptly, and this time he's not pushing me away—no—this time he's all in, coaxing my mouth open with his tongue and kissing me with everything that he has.

The sound of my cell phone ringing again breaks me out of the haze. I place my hands on Luca's chest and give him a light shove.

"I'm sorry." I say the words I don't mean; I want this, want him, but I'm fighting what I feel, shrouded in confusion.

"It's okay, Ev."

"Oh my God, what is happening to me? What am I doing?"

He places his forefinger underneath my chin and tilts my head up until our eyes are locked.

"You're waking up; you're realizing that you have feelings for me."

"I'm married, Luca," I tell him with very little conviction. We both know that my marriage is over, and I'm looking for permission to cross over that line.

"Yeah, you got married, but you don't have a husband, and you need to accept that things are happening with Tyler that have all of his attention. He's out of control, and he's never going to give you what you want. If you stay, he'll only drag you down with him."

"How did this happen, Luca, do you know?"

"You have to ask him, Everly. He's been placing bets as long as I've known him, but it was never anything like this."

"Maybe I should go for now." I quickly stand and move to walk away, but he grabs my hand and pulls me to him. He uses his free hand to grab me by the nape of my neck, and his lips are on mine. My brain is telling me to push him away, to put an end to what's happening between us, but I can't. I don't want to, everything inside of me is telling me that this is right, he feels right. We pull apart slowly, and I stare at him eyes wide, scared, shocked, needy.

"Luca." I say his name barely above a whisper because, even though I know I'm out of control, all of a sudden I feel like I've finally been found. "Why does this feel so familiar, like I've been missing you and I didn't even know it?"

"Maybe you wanted me all along, maybe you buried your feelings for me, maybe you thought you hated me because you believed I didn't return those feelings."

"I wanted you."

"It's not too late. If you're honestly done with Tyler, then it's not too late for us."

"What about your friendship? Are you willing to throw that away?"

"Tyler knows how I feel about you, Everly. He's not stupid, he's always known, and the truth is that you should have always been with me."

"Luca," I whisper, my heart racing.

"I saw you in that bookstore, and I wanted you from that moment on. I hated that you were with him, but even though you were, in my mind, I always felt like I had this fucked-up claim on you. He knew how I felt about you, and he went after you anyway."

"Wait, what? How? Luca, I met Tyler a few days after you. I never saw you after the bookstore. How could he have known?"

"You didn't see me, but I saw you, Ev. My biggest mistake was not making my move when I first met you. I thought I'd get another chance, and I didn't want to come on too strong."

"You liked me?" I question in disbelief.

"Baby, I went home afterward and told Ty about you, told him how I met this girl, the most beautiful girl. That night we went to a frat party, it was crazy and crowded, but I spotted you again. I pointed you out to him just as you were leaving. He told me I should go after you, but I told him no, you had already left. I figured it was a small campus and I'd see you again once classes started."

"Oh, my God."

"I never thought you'd have a class with him, and he'd make a move on you. I never thought he'd take you knowing how I felt."

"Luca," I whisper, tears swimming in my eyes. "I didn't know. I swear to you, I liked you, too. I wanted you to ask me for my number, I wanted you first. I just thought...and then I met him, and he was sweet, charismatic, it was hard not to like him. I was shocked that first time I went to your place and I saw you there, but I thought that at least we could be friends. Well, you know how well that worked out."

"I should have been better to you. It wasn't your fault, but if you would have shown me just once while you were with him that you cared about me, even a little, I would have gone after you, and it would have fucked my friendship with Ty up but I think at this point it's too late."

"I get it now," I say stroking his cheek. "I'm sorry it happened. I'm sorry he did that to you."

"All's fair in love and war, but I'll tell you right now." He pushes a strand of hair from my face. "I'm not letting you go again."

"I don't want you to let me go," I answer honestly, "but legally I'm still married."

"Do you still love him?"

"I think a part of me will always love him. He's played a huge part in my life, but there's been so much damage, so many lies, Luca. When he started to check out on me, I guess I started to check out emotionally on him, too. My feelings have changed, and I can't go back to how it was before. I know too much, I've seen too much."

"Stay, stay with me. We don't have to do anything. It's late, we'll just go to sleep and see how we feel in the morning."

"Okay," I agree, bringing my forehead to rest on his chest. He wraps his arms around my waist and pulls me closer, providing the comfort I'm desperately seeking. He pulls back slightly, kisses the top of my head, and leads me into the bedroom. We get into bed together, me on my side and him behind me enveloping me in his arms. I can't deny the guilt I feel for being here, the vows that I took that are all but broken, but

59

the fact that I married Tyler doesn't negate what I'm feeling for Luca. It's real; this isn't something that happened overnight. The feelings are not new; they've merely been suppressed by the fear of rejection.

We both wanted each other way back in the beginning, back four years ago in that crowded little bookstore, and if I had known that he felt the same back then, I would have chosen him. I would have wanted Luca. Tyler became a roadblock in the course I would have chosen to take, and I don't regret it, but now it's time for me to choose for myself. And as hard as it is, I chose Luca.

I know what people will think. I know what they'll say, but when I took those vows with Tyler, I meant them. I believed in them, and I wanted them to be true. But they were based on a life that wasn't real. Tyler was not the man that he presented himself as and I can't force myself to live the lie. If that makes me a bitch then so be it. If people think I'm wrong, then so be it; it's easy to judge someone when you haven't experienced their pain. So I close my eyes and let myself be held, be cared for by someone who wants to put me first, someone who chooses me over what others might think, and I do it knowing that it's the right thing for me.

❧

-I want a divorce -

I stare at the text for so long that the words start to blend together. I scrub my face with the palm of my hands trying to wrap my brain around what's happening. It's not that I'm shocked that it's come to this; I knew it was coming, but I'm shocked that Tyler is the one to have initiated it. We haven't spoken since I left the house three days ago, and I've been trying to figure out what to do, how to go about putting my unraveled life back together. I thought about filing for divorce, but I wanted to give it time. I wanted to give Tyler a chance to dig himself out of the hole he's in before I threw anything else onto his plate. I didn't want to make it worse, but I guess he beat me to the punch. I type out a response and hit send.

- Do you want to talk about things? -

- No. This is for the best. I need to get my shit together and you can't be a part of that. The best thing I can do for you is set you free. I'll take care of the paperwork I don't want you to worry about it. –

I don't respond because there's nothing left to say. Life is messy, it gets ugly, and this is the shitty hand I was dealt. Now, it's time to clean it up and this is the first step. Tyler needs help beyond what I can do for him right now; he needs something that my love alone can't give him especially now.

"Ev, you ready?" Luca calls from the living room. I toss my phone in my bag and make my way out to him.

"I'm ready," I say reaching the living room. For the last two days, we've been going on mini outings aka dates to get coffee, the movies, and now dinner. It's our way of taking things slow and being respectful, even though at times we just want to rip each other's clothes off.

"You look beautiful, baby," he tells me, and I melt because Luca makes me feel beautiful in a way that no one ever has. It's the way he looks at me, like no one else exists, like no one else can compare to me, and I love it. He takes my hand and leads me out to his car, a cherry red pickup truck; he opens my door and waits till I've buckled my belt before closing it.

"You good with Italian," he questions, fastening his own seatbelt.

"Sounds good."

He turns up the music, and we drive in silence. It gives me the chance to think through what's just happened and come to terms with how drastically my life has changed. When we reach the restaurant, Luca comes around and helps me out of the car; he holds my hand and leads me inside. The strangeness of this is not lost on me—being here with my husband's best friend—and how it would look to anyone who knows us.

"Ev? How are you doing with everything that you've learned in the last few weeks?" Luca asks after we are seated and have placed our orders. I sip on my sweet red wine mulling the question over in my head.

"I'm dealing with it, starting to process that things weren't always what they seemed."

"I am sorry you know." I hear the sincerity in his voice, and I know he wouldn't have wanted me to go through this upheaval, but none of this was in his control.

"I know you are and this helps."

"I'm glad."

"I just... Every day I wake up and I hope to see something different. I hope that it was all just a bad dream and then I realize it's not and I can't help but wonder if I made a mistake."

"A mistake how?"

"A mistake in falling in love with the wrong man."

"Ev..."

"He loves me, Luca. I know that, I have *never* doubted that not even once. But he also lied, and I deserved to know the truth and there are times when I think that I deserved more. I deserved someone who could be honest, someone who would love me enough to trust me. I would never have judged him. He has an addiction, and I can see that. I can rationalize it, and I would have stood by him. But I would have liked to do it with eyes wide open. I didn't deserve what I got."

"No you didn't."

"He's filing for divorce," I tell him as I finger the rim of my wine glass.

"He's doing what?"

"Yeah, he sent me a text earlier. He said it was for the best."

"How do you feel about that?" he probes.

"I'm sad but I agree. I would have probably waited a little while to spare his feelings, but we based everything on lies and it's hard to move on from that."

He nods, seemingly satisfied by my answer. "I can understand that."

"You're not a rebound, you know? I don't want you to think that I'm trying to pick up the next guy I saw after my marriage blew up in my face."

He gives me a chuckle and a confident smirk. "I know that, baby."

I smile back at him, loving how easygoing he is, how he takes everything as it comes and makes it possible for me to maneuver through the messiness of my life.

We make it back to Luca's apartment, and I throw my purse down on the kitchen table before turning to face him.

"I was thinking that maybe I should go stay with Morgan for a while."

He removes his jacket, tossing it on a chair. "Why?"

"This thing between us is new. I'm not divorced yet, and I don't want it to fizzle out or outstay my welcome because we didn't take things slow."

"I've wanted you for four years; how much slower can we get?" he says, walking over to me.

"You know what I mean," I declare with very little conviction.

"Let's talk about this later," he says grabbing onto my hips and pulling me to him. His lips are on mine again, and I'm done—done thinking and done fighting. If I'm going down, I'm going with this man who I've secretly and subconsciously wanted all along. I go up on my toes to give him better access and cling to him as though my life depends on it. His hands move down my body, grazing my ass and reaching the back of my thighs to haul me up. I wrap my legs around his hips, never breaking the kiss, and the next thing I know we're on the move. Luca is walking through a doorway and then we're down on his bed, me on my back and him on top of me.

My hands are everywhere, tugging his shirt off and desperately exploring the muscles of his back, his hips, his thighs, trying to make myself familiar with every part of him at the same time giving him permission to do the same. His hand rests on my stomach and slowly begins to slide up and underneath my shirt, his touch warming me all over. His thumb swipes at the swell of my breast and my back arches involuntarily, a moan escaping my lips. His fingers graze my nipple, causing a rush of wetness to gather between my legs. It's never been like this before, where I so recklessly abandon all self-control, where my only focus is on maximizing the sensations and nothing else. He breaks the kiss, and I cry out at the loss of him, I don't want this to stop. He looks down at me, his face serious but the desire in his eyes is unmistakable. He wants me as much as I want him.

"Everly, I'm giving you two seconds to get up and walk out of here before I rip your clothes off and bury myself inside of you."

His mouth is so close that all I can think of is getting it on me. I suck his lower lip, gently nipping at it before letting go. He needs me to reassure him of my decision. He needs to know that I want him, and I have no problem giving that to him. "I'm not going anywhere."

"Take your shirt off, Ev. Show me that you want this."

His voice is hypnotic and soothing, making me want to give him what he wants. Without hesitation I sit up, grabbing the hem of my t-shirt, and pull it over my head. His eyes focus on the black lace of my bra, just his look of lust and hunger sends a jolt of electricity through me. He runs a finger over the scalloped edges of my bra before pulling the cups down to expose my breasts to him completely. There's no time to protest because his mouth is on me almost instantly, sucking on one breast while working the other one with his fingers, tugging and circling my nipples and making me cry out in pleasure.

"Luca, please," I whimper, not recognizing my own voice. I sound desperate and needy, and at the moment, that's exactly how I feel. I can't get him close enough; every touch just leaves me wanting more.

He responds by lifting his torso up and off me, undoing the button on my pants, and tugging them down my legs leaving me in only my underwear. I reach around my back to unfasten the clasp of my bra and shrug it off. I've only been this exposed for one other person, and right now, the man standing in front of me blurs all thoughts of him.

"You're so fucking beautiful," he says, eyes locked on mine.

I'm breathless now, panting for air as his hands go to the waist of his pants. He has them down his legs and off before I can move, and I barely make out the sound of them hitting the floor. The sight of him takes me aback—his bare chest, broad shoulders, and the beautiful muscles that line his abs. My gaze travels down, and I swear I can feel my heart rate quicken. Luca is beautiful, from head to toe, completely and utterly blessed.

He leans down, placing a kiss on my lips, his hand down my panties causing me to whimper into his mouth. His finger slides through the folds of my wet pussy and my body convulses.

The feeling of him caressing me is mind-blowing, almost too much to handle, but I crave it, need more of him, as much as he can give.

"Fuck, baby, you're so wet for me."

"Condom," is all I can manage to get out of my mouth. He reaches over to his nightstand, pulls out a condom, and quickly rolls it on.

"You're ready?" he asks looking down at me again.

"Yes."

He pulls my panties down and off in a split second, a gust of cold air hits my naked body before he's over me again, covering me with his body, and kissing me again.

"Last chance, baby."

"Please, Luca," I beg, and he positions himself between my legs, his hard cock at my entrance, making me want him all the more. I jut my hips up to let him know exactly what I want, and thankfully, he's in the mood to give me exactly what I want. He growls as he slides in, filling me up and making me cry out at the initial shock of him there.

"Fuck, you're tight," he strains out.

I feel free, I feel alive, and moments like these are rare in my life as of late. He looks down at me, assessing the situation, and I can feel the tension in his muscles. His need to make sure I'm all right overshadows his need to move.

"You okay?"

"Yes," I reply, on a breath. I relax my muscles, allowing myself to acclimate to his size. I lift my head up to capture his lips with mine, tasting his tongue. I grip his shoulders to urge him to go on. Slowly, he begins to move his hips, and I throw my head back, savoring every single sensation that travels through me. Every thrust is like a conduit, lighting me up, setting me on fire, and making me beg for more.

I lift my legs and one by one wrap them around Luca's waist, deepening the connection even further. His cock feels impossibly large inside of me, stretching me to the max, enhancing the already intense sensations passing though me. He kisses and suckles at my neck and starts to increase his pace, thrusting his cock harder and faster with every passing moment. I circle my hips, doing my best to meet his movements; I can barely register the sound of my own cries as my pleasure intensifies. I know it's coming, the buildup of pressure starting in my stomach and shooting out to my nerve endings. He groans in my ear, and I know he's close.

"Oh fuck, Everly."

"Harder," I cry, and he complies, thrusting with a relentless rhythm making me delirious. I feel like I'm breaking apart into a million tiny pieces, and I welcome it. I need him to shatter me in order to make me whole again. Our lips crash together again, tongues tangle, and with one final push of his hips, I'm coming undone falling down a spiral of bliss so huge I don't know if I'll ever recover. Luca collapses on top of me, and I hold tight to him as his release shoots into me. I hear his grunt of pleasure and can feel the pulse of his cock as he comes, leaving me sated and spent.

Luca nuzzles my nose with the tip of his. "Jesus Christ."

I close my eyes, enjoying the aftershocks of pleasure, and his lips on my mouth, my chin, my neck. I hear him let out a sigh, and I whimper as he slides out of me. He kisses me one last time.

"I'll be right back." He moves out of the bed and walks into the bathroom in order to discard the condom. I close my eyes, letting myself relax and not allowing myself even a moment to think about or regret what just happened. A few minutes later, the bed depresses. My eyes flutter open, and I'm looking up at Luca's beautiful face.

"Open your legs, baby," he commands softly. My pussy spasms at the sound of his words, but I do as he asks and spread for him. He uses a warm rag to clean me up, tossing it on the floor once he's done. He climbs back into bed, settles into his pillows, wraps an arm around my waist, and pulls me into his body. I like this, like how it feels to be in his arms and in his bed, so I rest my head on his chest, my arm around his waist and relax into him. I close my eyes, and strangely enough, it doesn't take long for me to let go and fall into a peaceful dreamless sleep.

The sun is beaming down on me, and I can feel it on my skin through my closed eyelids. Why didn't I shut the blinds? I'm feeling a little parched, overheated like I'm wrapped up in heavy blankets. I take a minute and open my eyes, looking out the window... not my window. I look down on a sharp intake of breath to find that I'm completely naked. I'm about to freak when I feel movement behind me, an arm thrown over then tightening around my waist...Luca.

The events of last night come flooding back—our date, us coming back here and making love.

"I know you're awake, Ev."

I catch my breath at the sound of his voice then slowly turn around to face him. He looks unreal first thing in the morning—hair tousled, sleepy eyes, and a sexy grin. My heart flutters just looking at him. "Hi," I whisper.

He smiles at me, sending a rush of warmth right through me. He looks happy that I'm here and that thought makes a little bit of my embarrassment fall away. "Hi." His lips come down to mine, and he gives me a chaste kiss.

I use his silence as my opening. "Luca."

He cuts me off with another kiss, this one deeper, hotter. And just like that, I want him again. I open my eyes when he breaks the kiss to find him smiling again. He clearly sees the humor in this situation.

"Babe, whatever's running through your mind right now, let it go. We had a good time last night, and that's all that matters."

"No, I know. It's just that…"

"Just what?" he probes, pushing a strand of hair behind my ear.

"I've never really done this before, I've only been with one other person. I'm not sure what happens now."

He pushes slightly off me, still hovering but now looking more than inviting.

"You feel something for me, and I know sure as shit that I feel something for you. This wasn't about just fun, but it also doesn't have to be so complicated. This was us breaking down a barrier, and now we can explore what's between us."

His reply scares me while at the same time making me happy. How do I reconcile the fact that a few months ago I thought I hated this man? And now I'm here occupying his bed and wanting so badly for it to not end. "This is bad."

"What?" he questions, shaking his head.

"Oh shit." I'm panicking; so many obstacles stand in the way of Luca and me developing a relationship. He's my husband's best friend. I have a husband, and I know that I left him last night and technically I'm free to move on with whoever I want, but I know how people talk and I don't want to deal with that.

"Everly, don't go there."

"But…"

"No, we did nothing wrong. You walked away from him, and you ended it. Have you changed your mind?"

"No."

"Then we're fine."

"Luca." It's a plea. I need him to untangle the mess in my head, to unravel the ball of knots in my stomach and tell me that everything is going to be all right, that we can get to know each other without worrying about what the potential for disaster is.

"We did nothing wrong," he says again. He cups my chin with his hand forcing me to look him in the eye. "I want you, you want me; he asked for a divorce, there's nothing to stand in our way. If I have to, I'll handle Tyler."

"Okay," I breathe out, feeling slightly better.

"Are we good?"

I nod my head, and his forehead drops to mine. His eyes are heated, and his voice is husky as his hand slips down my torso and cups my sex. "We don't have to figure anything out today." His fingers find my already swollen clit and start circling. Instinctively, my hand comes up and I hold onto his neck, keeping him connected to me. "All that we need to do today is this. Enjoy what we have right now."

"Yes." I sigh, loving the feel of his hands on me.

His lips come down possessively, taking mine in his, and suddenly, I'm all for his plan for the day. In fact, his plan for the day is exactly what I want.

For the next two days, Luc and I are literally inseparable, both of us barely getting out of bed. We are living in a bubble of our own creation, and it's been amazing. Our bubble burst this morning when Luca was called into work. He's been doing per diem hours at a local law firm, and he couldn't say no. I decided to use the free time to go to my house and pack more of my things since I've been walking around in nothing but Luca's t-shirt for the past few days. I pull into the driveway instead of the garage since I'm not planning to stay for more than a few minutes. I barely make it out of the car before I sense someone behind me. I turn to find two men I've never seen before standing in my driveway, two huge men.

"Mrs. West?"

"Yes, can I help you?"

"We're looking for your husband, Mrs. West."

"He's not here, and I haven't seen him in days. Can I give him a message?"

"Yeah, we have a message."

I never see it coming. His fist connects with my jaw, and I'm down, my head barely misses the concrete as I cry out in pain.

"Wait," I plead. "Please, I don't know anything." I try to get off the ground but one of them pushes me down while the other one kicks me. He shows no mercy as the metal tip of his boot connects with my gut. The pain is so sharp that it radiates through me, like being stabbed with a knife. He kicks me again and again, and I think I may pass out from the pain. I'm not sure how long it goes on, but I'm filled with relief when it finally stops, only to have him pull me up to my knees by my hair. His face is close to mine, not caring that I can see his face, not caring that he's likely broken a rib. There is no remorse, not on either of their faces, and this is what Tyler has brought to our door.

"Tell your husband to come see us, Mrs. West, because if we have to come back, no one will be able to recognize that pretty little face of yours." He releases me and I fall to the ground never shedding a tear. I wait until I hear the sound of the car pulling away before struggling to my feet and picking up my purse from where it landed on the grass. I pull out my cell and search for the number hitting send once I've found it.

"Hey baby, you okay?"

"Luca, I need your help."

"Ev? What happened, what's wrong?"

I quickly recap what happened, and he loses it.

"Motherfucker. I'm going to kill Tyler myself. Get in the house, baby, lock the doors and stay away from any windows. I'm on my way, okay?"

"Okay, should I call Tyler?"

"No. You do not call him, and you do not speak to him if he comes to the house before I get there, you call the cops. I will handle Tyler."

"Okay, please hurry."

"I'm leaving now, baby."

Luca gets here in less than ten minutes; I've never been so relieved to see anyone. His anger is so palpable it almost takes on a life of its own, but he places a kiss on my forehead, gathers me into his arms, and carries me out of the house with barely a word spoken.

"Where are we going?" I question after he's positioned me in the already reclined passenger's seat and climbed behind the wheel.

"Hospital."

"Should we have called the cops?"

"Not here, baby. We don't know if they're watching the house. We'll get the cops to come to the hospital to get your statement."

"We should have stayed in bed," I tell him, trying to make light of the situation, but he's having none of it.

"This shit has to end. One way or another, this shit has to end."

It's been a week since I was attacked by the men who are after Tyler, a week since anyone has seen or heard from him except for a random text I got while I was in the hospital saying *I'm sorry.* He's made no other contact, and I'm scared for him, I truly am, but right now I can only focus on my own recovery, especially since it's clear that Tyler doesn't want to be helped.

I'm finally starting to feel a little bit better. My ribs were bruised pretty badly, but thankfully, nothing was broken. Thankfully, I was able to walk away with just a few minor bumps and bruises. The police have been patrolling Luca's street to make sure that we have at least a little bit of protection, but Luca seems to think that they won't come after us again. He thinks that they just wanted to send a message to Tyler, but I'm not so sure they're just going to leave us alone, especially me. My parents were frantic when they heard what was going on, and since I refused to go stay with them, they drop by Luca's house daily, as do his parents. It was hard for any of them to believe the mess that Tyler has made of things.

The sound of my cell phone ringing startles me. I had just dozed off on the couch moments before while watching a movie with Luca. I reach for the phone not recognizing the number on the display.

"Hello?" I answer, putting the call on speakerphone.

"Everly, where are you?"

"Tyler, where the hell have you been? Everyone is looking for you."

"I'm okay, This will all be over tomorrow, Ev. I got the money from my dad like you said; I finally went to him and got it. I'm so sorry for what happened to you, I never meant for you to get hurt."

"I know that, Ty."

"Where are you? Can I see you?"

"I'm with Luca, and I don't think that's a good idea."

Silence

"I see." His voice cracks but he recovers quickly. "That's good, Everly, that's where you should be. He'll take care of you; promise me that you'll stay there."

"I want to help you. You have to let me help you, Tyler, once you pay back the money. You need to see someone."

"I'm fine, I am, and Luca, he loves you—he always has."

"I know," I whisper, unable to hide the sadness I feel for him.

"I've really made a mess of things, huh?" he questions, his tone matching my own.

"Don't say that, you're sick. I know that, and now I understand that. I want you to get better, Ty, but I can't be around all of the chaos you've created."

"No, I know it's for the best. It always should have been this way, he wanted you first and I knew that, I knew that before you and I officially met. I just didn't care. I wanted you for myself, so I lied to him and I took you."

"It doesn't matter now; the only thing that matters now is that you get out of this mess."

"Tell him I'm sorry, Everly. I'm so sorry. Tell him that no matter what happens, I still love him like a brother."

"I love you too, man," Luca chimes in having heard the whole conversation. "Just get better; we can deal with everything else later."

"Yeah, goodbye." He hangs up the phone, and I think a part of me knows that I'll never speak to him again. Luca pulls me up gently, careful not to aggravate my bruises and places me on his lap.

"How are you doing?"

"I'm okay. I'm really scared for him, though. I really do want him to get help."

"He has to decide that for himself, baby."

"I know."

⁓⚮⁓

After two days with no further word from Tyler, I finally decide that I need to check on the house and get some of my clothes. I'll hire movers for the rest of my things once everything with Tyler has settled down. Luca, of course, being the man that he is wouldn't let me come alone so he demanded that he drive me. We pull into the garage and I let us in the house through the side door.

"Can you grab us some waters while I run upstairs and grab some clothes?"

"Sure," he says heading over to the refrigerator while I head upstairs to what once was my bedroom. It feels so strange to think of it as part of my past, but that's exactly what it's become. I open the door and gasp at the sight before me, my eyes go wide, and I suck in a deep breath. I can't think, can't process anything around me all I can do is stare at Tyler lying on the floor in a pool of blood. I shake my head slowly in disbelief, his eyes are closed, and his skin is pale, so pale.

"Oh, my God." I run over to him and fall to my knees as my body starts to tremble and my eyes glass over. *No, this can't be happening.* "Tyler?" I call out through tears. "Tyler, please... please," I beg. "You have to get up, Ty, we have to go." My eyes get blurrier with each passing moment.

I touch Tyler's cheek, and it feels hard, so cold, and I don't understand. I don't get it. I don't accept it.

"Please, Ty, don't do this. Why are you doing this?" I scream as I shake him harder. "No, no, no, no, no..." I scream, pushing off the floor and running into the hallway. I collapse in the hall and continue to cry and scream. I'm losing my mind, I have to be losing it. This isn't real; it's not possible.

"Jesus, Everly. What the fuck?"

"Luca, Luca, please, please help me," I cry through chattering teeth.

I look up at his stunned face.

"Okay Ev, I'm just going to help you up, okay?"

I'm numb; my whole body is numb. I don't feel his arms wrap around me as he helps me back into the room. I'm shocked and completely dazed. "Tyler," I cry.

Luca stares at the scene for a moment and nods slowly.

"Fuck."

I close my eyes and shudder. The tears rolling down my cheeks are the only thing I can feel. "Please, Luca. Please help him."

"Fuck," I hear Luca scream, and I jump back. I open my eyes, and he's hovering over Ty. *Why isn't he helping him?*

"Do something!" I screech. No longer able to control my tears. "Please..."

"Baby, he's been shot in the chest. He's gone."

Gone. Gone. *Tyler's gone.* Those are the last words I hear before my world goes **black and** before my entire life collapses around me. *Tyler's gone.*

Epilogue

"Everly." I hear someone call from a distance. "Everly, you have to wake up." *My mom, it sounds like my mom,* I think as my eyes flutter open.

"Everly." I hear again followed by a knock on the door. I shoot up in bed looking for Luca, looking for-

"Tyler," I whisper, remembering how I found his body only moments ago. I was with Luca and Tyler...

"Everly, you really have to get up."

"I'm coming," I call trying to figure out what's going on. I look around the room and a gush of air escapes from my lungs as I see it. My wedding dress hanging on the closet door.

"It was a dream?" I ask out loud, still feeling out of sorts, but it felt so real, everything about it felt real. I glance at my phone and look at the date, my wedding day to Luca, four years after Tyler was killed in the park, four years after my life fell apart. He didn't survive, but God, for a minute there I thought he had, for a minute there I thought the dream was real. I look down at my left hand and see the beautiful diamond on my ring finger. I'm engaged to Luca, I'm marrying Luca, and we're having a baby.

"Mom, I just need a minute. I overslept I'll be right down," I say in order to keep her from knocking again.

"Okay," she says as I pick up the phone again and call Luca.

"Good morning, baby."

"Hey, how was guys' night at the hotel."

"Very PG-13, I promise."

"Good."

"What's wrong, Ev?"

"I just had the strangest dream."

"What about?"

"I dreamt that Tyler survived, that you went to the park instead of him that day and you were shot, only you didn't die. You were hurt, though."

"Some dream."

"I know. But Luca, the dream was worse because instead of fixing things, Tyler just made them worse, he got you shot and he got me in the middle of things but you know what was the strangest part?"

"What?"

"You and I, we ended up together anyway. We found each other, no matter what, and we couldn't save him, Luca. Tyler died anyway."

"I think maybe Tyler's trying to tell you something."

"I think so, too," I say wiping a stray tear. "No matter how it would have all played out, no matter all the what if's we've asked ourselves over and over again things ended up as they should. We were going to find each other no matter what, weren't we?"

"Yes, baby."

"Okay."

"Feel better now?"

"Starting to, yes."

"Everly, we're a family. We were always meant to be that—you, me, and our little boy you're carrying."

I smile, taking in his words, and place a hand on my stomach.

"I still can't believe it."

"Believe it, baby. We deserve to be happy, that's what we do for each other and we're going to keep on doing it."

"He said I should be with you—in the dream, Tyler told me I should be with you. He said you'd take care of me; it's one of the last things he said."

"And I will—always. I promise you."

"I love you."

"I love you, too. I'll meet you at the altar; I'll be the one in the tux wearing a stupid grin on his face."

"Got it," I say with a giggle.

"See ya, baby."

"See ya," I reply before hanging up.

There have been so many times over the last few years, especially after Luca and I got together where I've asked myself what if? What if Tyler survived, what would have happened? Would he have gotten help or kept on his destructive path? Would we have made it or would I have found my way to Luca anyway? After the dream, I feel like all of those questions have been answered, I think Tyler was trying to tell me that I am exactly where I'm supposed to be. One way or another, I would have ended up with Luca, and I wouldn't have it any other way. He really is the love of my life.

"I did this for you," I mutter as my mother fixes my veil for the hundredth time today. "

"You look stunning," she tells me through watery eyes.

I'm fighting the anxiety as best as I can, but it's grabbing hold of me and I can't seem to shake it. "I don't know if I can do this."

"Honey." She turns me to face her and gives me her brilliant smile. "You have nothing to worry about."

"I wanted to get married at a courthouse, just me and Luca, but I did this for you... I did this to make you happy and now I'm freaking out."

"Everly."

"What if something goes wrong? What if..."

"What if what?" I hear from behind me somewhere inside the back room where I'm being stashed at the church.

I turn, only to come face to face with Luca, the man I love, the man of my dreams. One look at him and the panic and fear I've felt all day begins to recede.

"Baby," I call out to him, the relief in my voice is clear.

"Did you think I'd ditch you?"

I spot my mom out of the corner of my eye moving out of the room, and I release the gush of breath that I must have been holding and shake my head. "You're not supposed to see me in my dress."

"When this day is over, we'll be married. It'll be just us, me and you." He walks into the room and stops just a few feet away. "Once you walk down that aisle, I will not leave your side, and I won't let you go. I won't leave you alone; I will not go away... so whatever fear you're holding onto, you need to let it go because this is not that. This is our story, just you and me and the past cannot touch us anymore."

"It's not you leaving me that I'm afraid of, not by choice anyway."

"I'm not going to die, babe. Not today, anyway. I can't promise you that it'll never happen, that something won't happen to me one day, but what I can promise you is that you will never lose me to something that I could have prevented. You'll never lose me because I chose something else over you, over our baby. Can you live with that?"

"Yes. It's just hard to let you walk away from me sometimes."

"Today?"

I nod my confirmation, and he gets it. I know he understands my irrational fears, and I love him even more for not making me feel like I'm crazy.

"Come on. Let's go get married, Ev."

"Okay, you're right. I'll meet you at the altar," I tell him with a smile.

"No. You and I—we'll get to the altar together," he declares taking my hand and pulling me out of the room.

"What? Luca, what about my dad? He's waiting to walk me down the aisle."

He squeezes my hand and smiles. "He'll understand. We're having this wedding to make our family happy. They'll understand that we need to do this together, and they'll give us that much."

I stand by while Luca has a word with my father, who just nods and gives him a pat on the arm. My dad walks over to me and pulls me into his arms.

"I love you, sweetheart. Don't you worry, okay?"

"I love you too, Daddy," I tell him before he walks into the church and take his seat up front.

When the music begins and the double doors open, all of my fears, all of my doubts and worries fade away and all that's left is us. Luca and I, his hand holding mine, our baby growing inside of me, and it's perfect. The perfect ending to a difficult past, the perfect beginning to a beautiful life.

Unspeakable Lies

Made in the USA
Middletown, DE
18 May 2015